Reader's Clubhouse

W9-ARM-582

JUST THE RIGHT HOME

By Judy Kentor Schmauss
Illustrated by Marilee Harrald-Pilz

BARRON'S

Table of Contents

© Copyright 2006 by Barron's Educational Series, Inc.

Illustrations on pages 21 and 23 created by Carol Stutz

All inquiries should be addressed to:
Barron's Educational Series, Inc.
250 Wireless Boulevard
Hauppauge, New York 11788
www.barronseduc.com

Library of Congress Catalog Card No.: 2005053585

ISBN-13: 978-0-7641-3299-5
ISBN-10: 0-7641-3299-7

Library of Congress Cataloging-in-Publication Data
Schmauss, Judy Kentor.
    Just the right home / Judy Kentor Schmauss.
        p. cm. – (Reader's clubhouse)
    ISBN-13: 978-0-7641-3299-5
    ISBN-10: 0-7641-3299-7
    1. Dwellings—Juvenile literature. I. Title. II. Series.

TH4811.5.S35 2006
392.3'6—dc22

                                                                    2005053585

PRINTED IN CHINA
9 8 7 6 5 4 3 2

Dear Parent and Educator,

Welcome to the Barron's Reader's Clubhouse, a series of books that provide a phonics approach to reading.

Phonics is the relationship between letters and sounds. It is a system that teaches children that letters have specific sounds. Level 1 books introduce the short-vowel sounds. Level 2 books progress to the long-vowel sounds. This progression matches how phonics is taught in many classrooms.

Just the Right Home reviews the long "i," "o," and "u" sounds introduced in previous Level 2 books. Simple words with these long-vowel sounds are called **decodable words.** The child knows how to sound out these words because he or she has learned the sounds they include. This story also contains **high-frequency words.** These are common, everyday words that the child learns to read by sight. High-frequency words help ensure fluency and comprehension. **Challenging words** go a little beyond the reading level. The child will identify these words with help from the illustration on the page. All words are listed by their category on page 24.

Here are some coaching and prompting statements you can use to help a young reader read *Just the Right Home:*

- **On page 4, "home" is a decodable word. Point to the word and say:**

  Read this word. How did you know the word? What sounds did it make?

  Note: There are many opportunities to repeat the above instruction throughout the book.

- **On page 16, "wood" is a challenging word. Point to the word and say:**

  Read this word. It rhymes with "stood." How did you know the word? Did you look at the picture? How did it help?

You'll find more coaching ideas on the Reader's Clubhouse Web site: *www.barronsclubhouse.com.* Reader's Clubhouse is designed to teach and reinforce reading skills in a fun way. We hope you enjoy helping children discover their love of reading!

Sincerely,

Nancy Harris

Nancy Harris
Reading Consultant

We need a new home.

Come help us look for one.

Could this be the right home
for us? It is a boat.

This home might be just right.
We can float all around in it.

Could this be the right home
for us? It is made from stone.

This home might be just
right. We can draw on its
huge stones.

Could this be the right
home for us? It has a nice,
wide moat.

This home might be just right.
We can swim and float in
the moat.

Could this be the right home
for us? It has a spruce grove.

This home might be just right. We can climb up its spruce trees.

Could this be the right home
for us? It has a long drive.

This home might be just right.
We can hike up its long drive.

Could this be the right home
for us? It is made of dried
wood and twine.

This home might be just right.
We can slide down the vines.

Look! Look at this home!
What a stroke of good luck!

This home is just fine.
This home is just right!

Fun Facts About
Houses and Homes

- There are 132 rooms in the White House in Washington, D.C., the home of the President of the United States. How many rooms does *your* home have?

- Do you think your bedroom is too small? The sizes of most houses have almost doubled in the last 30 years. So if you were a kid 30 years ago, your room might have been half the size it is now!

- The biggest house in the world is the Chateau de Versailles in France. It was built for King Louis XIV. Because the house was so big, it took 50 years to build—from 1661 to 1710. The main building has 700 rooms!

- As indoor bathrooms became popular in the 1850s, families would convert an entire bedroom in their home to a large, grand bathroom.

- Here are some rooms you will find in most houses or apartments. Does your home look like this?

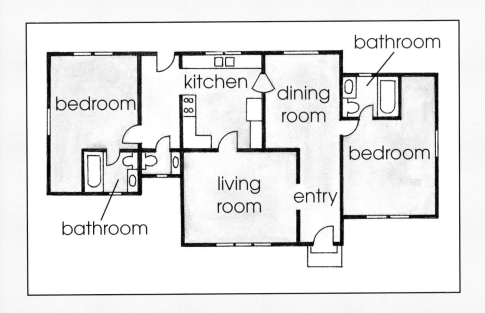

Log Cabin

You will need:

- construction paper (white and at least one other color)
- white glue or a glue stick
- child-safe scissors
- craft sticks
- crayons

1. Glue the craft sticks to the paper to make the wall of the cabin.

2. Cut a triangular roof for the cabin and cut off the point. Glue the roof to the paper above the wall.

3. Cut a rectangular door and square window.

4. Glue the door and window to the cabin.

5. Draw a doorknob and a background.

6. You can add a chimney, trees, and other details if you'd like.

Word List

Challenging Words	wood		
Decodable Long I, O, U Words	boat dried drive fine float grove hike home	huge might moat nice right slide spruce	stone stones stroke twine vines wide
High-Frequency Words	a all and around at be can climb come could down draw	for from good has help in is it its just long look	made new of on one the this up us we what